Buddy's Special Mission

By
Colleen Driscoll

Illustrated by
Kelsey Musgrave

This book belongs to Charlotte Clay, Age 2.
♥ Aunt Cindy

Buddy's Special Mission

by Colleen Driscoll

illustrated by Kelsey Musgrave

Additional copies of this book are available from Amazon.com, CreateSpace.com, and other retail outlets

To contact the author:

Email: cdriscollauthor@yahoo.com
www.cdriscollauthor.wixsite.com/colleendriscoll

CreateSpace, Charleston, SC.

ISBN: 1546602909
ISBN-13: 978-1546602903

DEDICATION

For Paul, JJ, & Raymond
In tribute to the military's
valiant fight and sacrifice
in defending our freedoms

Bacon? Do I smell bacon? Oh, boy! Andy is making a yummy breakfast. Today is going to be a great day. Wait a second. No, it's not. Today is the day he goes away. He gave me a mission to watch his family. Andy's mate will be easy to watch, but the little pup never rests. I don't know where my owner is going, but he packed his toothbrush and clothes—that's never a good sign.

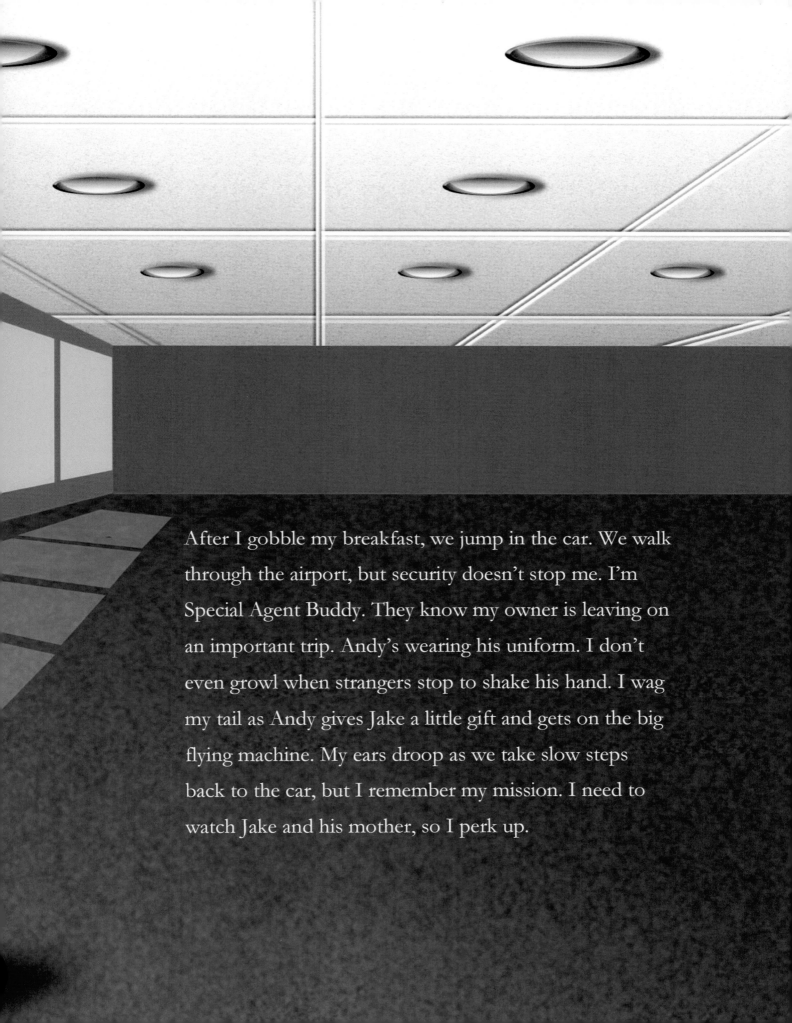

After I gobble my breakfast, we jump in the car. We walk through the airport, but security doesn't stop me. I'm Special Agent Buddy. They know my owner is leaving on an important trip. Andy's wearing his uniform. I don't even growl when strangers stop to shake his hand. I wag my tail as Andy gives Jake a little gift and gets on the big flying machine. My ears droop as we take slow steps back to the car, but I remember my mission. I need to watch Jake and his mother, so I perk up.

At home, Jake shows his mother the gift Andy gave him. "The flag is very important to Daddy," she says. "Why don't you keep it on the nightstand? You can think of Daddy when you look at it."

I leap on Jake's lap and bark. I miss Andy, too. Jake pretends to build schools and roads with his wooden blocks. "Why does Daddy help people rebuild their towns?" he asks.

"They need our help," she says. "People should always take care of each other."
I stand up and nudge my nose against Jake's leg. Don't worry, Jake. Special Agent Buddy will watch out for you.

Sometimes Jake and his mother talk on the computer.

I hear Andy's voice, but I can't
see him. I chew on my stick as
Jake tells stories about our day.

In the summer, we take daytrips and visit friends. Grandma and Poppy visit in July and bring me yummy peanut butter treats. Jake runs around the yard while I bark at the twinkling lights in the sky.

Sometimes Jake takes me to a big room with other children whose parents are away on duty. They talk about their feelings. Jake shows them his little flag.

I can tell when he feels sad. His bottom lip juts out, and he wipes his eyes. I sit next to him, and he pets me. When the other kids look sad, I rest my head on their laps. I feel calmer when they pet me, too.

When Jake goes back to school, I protect his mother when she cleans the house. I attack the noisy monster that cleans the carpet. I eat the food that spills on the floor. And I bark at the cars and dogs. I hear everything. I am a good guard dog. In the afternoon, I nap so I'm ready when Jake comes home.

When the weather turns cooler, Jake and his mother rake
the leaves in the yard. They gather them into a pile, and I
jump in. Swoosh! The leaves fly everywhere. Jake and his
mother shout, "Buddy!" Then they jump in the leaves, too. I
bark as they giggle. I like when we have fun.

Some days, Jake and I go for long walks. He lets me pee on the fire hydrants and sniff the grass to explore the neighborhood. Special Agent Buddy works hard to keep my family safe.

One morning, Jake puts on his Cub Scout uniform. We march in a parade behind a band playing loud music. Older people dressed in fancy uniforms walk down the street. My ears go back, and I stay close to Jake as the people cheer for us.

On quiet evenings, we look through the family photo albums.

"You look just like Daddy," Jake's mother says.

Jake grins. "Who's this?" he asks.

"That's your great-grandpa. He served in the military, too," she says. "When he was in the war trying to protect our country, he injured his leg."

Jake studies the picture more closely. "What medal is he holding?"

"The Purple Heart," she says.

I jump on the chair to see the brave man.

When Jake is home from school, we make videos to send to Andy. Jake helps his mother make cookies. The smell makes me drool. I eat the crumbs on Jake's shirt. They pack goodies and movies into a box, and I go with them to the post office.

At night, I nuzzle next to Jake as he rubs my belly. He holds his flag and tells me his daddy is a hero. I listen to him breathe as he sleeps. The peaceful sounds put me to sleep, but I miss Andy's loud snores.

As the weather gets colder, we stay inside the warm, cozy house. When the snow falls, Jake takes me outside. I love eating the fluffy white stuff. I could stand outside all day and sniff the fresh air. I run while he rolls snowballs and makes snowmen. I bark when he gets out the sled. I jump on his lap, and we ride down the hill. Whee!

The snow melts, and the days get warmer. One afternoon, Jake steps off the school bus. I leap on him and lick his face. He says, "Get down," but I can't calm down. I have a surprise to show him. I jump until he opens the front door. He stops in the doorway.

Surprise! My owner is inside. I dance in
circles as Jake runs to him.
"Daddy, you're home!"
Andy lifts him high in the air and laughs.
"Yes, I'm home." Andy reaches down and
rubs behind my ears. "Good boy, Buddy."
I wag my tail and give him a slobbery kiss.

After Jake goes to sleep, I sneak on Andy's lap and curl up with him. He pets my head and says, "Thank you for looking after our family while I was away." I put my paws on his chest and rest my head. My mission is complete.

Made in the USA
Middletown, DE
13 August 2017